Time Jumpers

ESCAPE FROM EGYPT

by
WENDY MASS

illustrated by
ORIOL VIDAL

BRANCHES

SCHOLASTIC INC.

Read all the

scholastic.com/timejumpers

Table of Contents

For the Diblings — I'd travel through

time to find you. —WM

To our beloved kitten, Lana. We'll miss

her "meows." —OV

Text copyright © 2018 by Wendy Mass
Illustrations by Oriol Vidal copyright © 2018 by Scholastic Inc.

Library of Congress Cataloging-in-Publication Data

Names: Mass, Wendy, 1967- author. | Vidal, Oriol, 1977- illustrator.
Title: Escape from Egypt / by Wendy Mass ; illustrated by Oriol Vidal.
Description: First edition. | New York : Branches/Scholastic Inc., 2018. | Series: Time Jumpers ; 2 | Summary: Ava and Chase want some more information before they embark on another adventure in time, but the woman who gave them the suitcase filled with magical objects is not being helpful, and when Chase picks up the scarab of King Tutankhamen they find themselves transported not to ancient Egypt, but to Egypt on the day King Tut's tomb is discovered—and they must get the artefact back into the tomb while avoiding Randall, who has arrived before them.
Identifiers: LCCN 2018002081 | ISBN 9781338217391 (pbk) | ISBN 9781338217407 (hjk)
Subjects: LCSH: Tutankhamen, King of Egypt—Tomb—Juvenile fiction. | Time travel—Juvenile fiction. | Scarabs—Juvenile fiction. | Magic—Juvenile fiction. | Adventure stories. | Egypt—Antiquities—Juvenile fiction. | Egypt—History—1919-1952—Juvenile fiction. | CYAC: Tutankhamen, King of Egypt—Tomb—Fiction. | Time travel—Fiction. | Scarabs—Fiction. | Magic—Fiction. | Adventure and adventurers—Fiction. | Egypt—Antiquities—Fiction. | Egypt—History—1919-1952—Fiction. | LCGFT: Action and adventure fiction.
Classification: LCC PZ7.M42355 Es 2018 | DDC 813.54 [Fic]
—dc23 LC record available at https://lccn.loc.gov/2018002081

10 9 8 7 6 5 4 3 2 1   18 19 20 21 22

Printed in China 62
First edition, November 2018
Illustrated by Oriol Vidal
Edited by Katie Carella
Book design by Sunny Lee

Shake, Rattle, and Roll

Chase presses his pillow over his head. It still doesn't drown out the noise coming from the suitcase under his bed. The sound had been getting louder and louder all night.

What a long, strange day! Earlier, he and Ava had met a woman named Madeline at the flea market. She gave them an old suitcase with many strange objects inside. But when they touched one of the objects, they jumped back in time to King Arthur's castle!

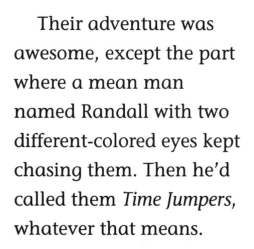

Their adventure was awesome, except the part where a mean man named Randall with two different-colored eyes kept chasing them. Then he'd called them *Time Jumpers*, whatever that means.

The pillow is suddenly yanked off Chase's head.

"I can hear that suitcase banging around all the way from my room!" Ava says in a loud whisper.

"Try sleeping above it," Chase grumbles. Ava grabs the suitcase.

Chase scrambles out of bed. "Ava! We agreed not to open it yet. We need to be prepared before we travel through time again. We have to ask Madeline what it means to be a Time Jumper."

"I know," Ava replies. But she is already opening the lid. "I won't touch anything. I just want to know what is making all this noise."

Chase has to admit he's curious, too.

The answer is clear right away. The black stone beetle with the green hexagon-shaped jewel on its back is popping out of its slot! Chase reaches over to push the beetle back into place. As soon as his fingertip grazes it, he realizes his mistake. Ava gasps and yanks his hand away.

It's too late. The room has already started to spin! Ava grabs for Chase's pajama sleeve, catching it just before the room fades away.

"Nooooo!" Chase shouts as he squeezes his eyes shut. "We're not ready!"

A Sandy Surprise

chapter 2

Heat, sand, and wind hit Chase and Ava from all sides.

"Where are we?" Chase shouts over the roar. "Why can't I feel the ground?"

"You have to see this!" Ava shouts back. "It's amazing!"

Chase opens his eyes and his jaw drops. He instantly gets a mouthful of sand! He spits it out and yelps, "We're in the desert!"

Well, not *in* the desert, exactly. More like hanging in the air ten feet *above* the desert. In the distance, Chase can see the tops of pyramids rising above the sandstorm.

Pyramids!

He risks another grainy mouthful to shout, "We're in ancient Egypt! The beetle in the suitcase must be a scarab beetle. It was a symbol of strength and power back then. We must need to do something with it or else we wouldn't have landed here."

"We haven't actually *landed* anywhere," Ava points out.

Chase looks down, then wishes he hadn't. "Whoa! What is *that?*"

A scorpion the size of his face is crawling across the sand!

Suddenly, they're swept up on the wind again. Chase grabs for Ava's hand. "Get ready to run *away* from the scorpion when we land!" he shouts. But instead of hitting the soft sand, they land on the hard wooden floor of Chase's bedroom.

Thump!

Ava sits up and sand flies from her hair. "What happened?" she asks. "Last time we traveled back in time, we only got home after we returned the object that sent us to the past."

"Maybe we came right back this time because my finger only touched the beetle for one second?" Chase suggests. "I never actually held it."

Ava nods. "That must be it," she said. "Hey, at least we got a sneak peek of where we're going next!"

Chase grins and grabs a book on the history of Egypt off his shelf. "Yes, and now we know what to bring!"

"Chase?" Mom calls from her room. "Are you still up?"

Ava shoves the suitcase back under the bed and dashes to her room.

"Going to sleep right now, Mom," Chase calls out. And if the suitcase would stop rattling, that would be a lot easier!

Looking for Answers

"Get them while they're hot," Dad says, setting his famous waffles on the table. "I'm going to wake up Mom." He heads upstairs.

Chase dives in before Ava can take all the waffles.

"Did the suitcase keep you up all night?" Ava asks Chase as she smothers her waffles with syrup. She is wearing the tie-dyed tutu and sunglasses she got at the flea market yesterday.

"I was too excited to sleep! So I looked up how to turn bedsheets into ancient Egyptian robes. We'll fit right in!" Chase says. "I just wish we didn't have to wait so long to talk to Madeline again. The next flea market is a whole week away, but we need answers now."

"We can get our answers *right now*!" Ava says, waving a small notebook in the air. "I found Madeline's address — and we can bike to it!"

"Good job!" Chase says as they dig into their breakfast.

"Hey, where did all the waffles go?" Mom asks, joining them at the table.

"Oops, sorry," Ava says, swallowing the last bite.

"Is it okay if we go for a bike ride?" Chase asks.

"Make sure you stay on the sidewalks," their mom says sleepily. Maybe the rattling kept her up last night, too!

"Should we bring the suitcase?" Ava asks as they grab their bikes from the garage.

Chase shakes his head. "We can't take a chance that Madeline might want it back." He doesn't want to scare Ava, so he doesn't mention his bigger worry: Randall. There is a special remote in the suitcase that they'd used to get home from King Arthur's castle. Chase knows Randall has a similar remote. When they left the castle, Randall was being taken to the king's dungeon. But if Randall had his remote with him, he could have escaped. . . .

Ava sings to herself as they bike across town. But Chase can't help sneaking peeks over his shoulder.

About twenty minutes into their ride, Ava stops and pulls a map from her basket. "I think we're lost. We're still all the way over here." She points to a street they'd passed a long time ago.

Chase shakes his head. "You're holding the map upside down."

"Ahh!" she says, rotating it. Then she points across the street. "That's Madeline's house right there!"

The house looks totally normal: two stories, a front porch, and kids' toys on the lawn. Chase feels a flash of disappointment. He'd expected something more mysterious.

Before they can ring the bell, a woman comes around the side of the house.

It's Madeline! She sees them and almost drops the flower box she's holding.

Chase's head swirls with all the questions he wants to ask her. His heart quickens. They're finally going to get some answers!

Spinning Tales

"Hello again," Madeline says. "I figured I hadn't seen the last of you two. Chase and Ava, right?"

"That's us!" Ava says.

Madeline's eyes flick down the street in both directions, then she waves for them to follow her to the backyard.

"Wait here." She points to a bench. "I'll get us some lemonade and we can talk."

17

The lemonade is refreshing after their long bike ride. Chase gulps it down, then asks, "Can you tell us where the suitcase you gave us came from?"

"My uncle brought it here a few months ago before he left for a business trip." She points to Chase's head. "He works at the Natural History Museum, where you got your hat. I hadn't meant to bring the suitcase to the flea market yesterday. It must've gotten mixed in with the other bags I was selling."

"Did you ever look inside?" Chase asks.

She shakes her head. "I couldn't get it open. Nothing rattled around when I shook it so I figured it was empty."

Chase and Ava share a look. It sure is rattling now!

"Why did you give it to us?" he asks.

"When I was growing up, my uncle told me a bedtime story about a brother and sister who could do magical things," she says softly. "I know it sounds crazy, but when the suitcase opened for you, and then I saw your dinosaur hat, I felt like maybe you were the kids from his story."

A chill goes down Chase's spine. Ava shivers, too.

"Why does Randall want the suitcase so badly?" Ava asks.

Madeline blinks. "Who's Randall?"

"You know, the guy who was yelling at you at the flea market?" Ava says. "Tall? Bald? Different-colored eyes? Bad breath?"

Leave it to Ava to notice his breath!

"Oh, *that* guy," Madeline says. "I never saw him before."

"But didn't he call you by your name?" Chase asks.

"And what are Time Jumpers?" Ava asks at the same time.

Madeline jumps up, knocking over her lemonade. "Sorry, I have to go." The back door bangs shut behind her.

"Well," Ava says. "That was super weird."

Chase nods. "At least we know a little more than when we got here," he says. "Let's go home. We've got a beetle to bring back in time!"

chapter 5

Picture This

Chase's legs ache from pedaling. He can't wait to get home! He'd packed the sheets and snacks. All he has left to do is fill the canteens they use on family hikes. They'll need a lot of water in the desert.

Ava catches up to him. "Do you think Madeline is right about us being the kids from her uncle's story? What if we're not and we mess everything up?"

"The suitcase opened for us," Chase points out. "I think that means we're the right ones."

"I hope so," Ava says.

They park their bikes and wave to their parents. "Let's duck inside before they ask for help with their latest art project," Ava whispers.

"Good idea," Chase replies. Last week he and Ava had spent three hours sorting tiny buttons into piles by color!

They can hear the suitcase as soon as they get upstairs. "That beetle clearly wants us to hurry up," Ava says.

Chase hands Ava the two canteens to fill, then plucks a paperback copy of *Egyptian History* from his bookshelf. He flips through it and gasps!

When Ava returns, he holds up the book so she can see the page. "Look at this!"

Her eyes widen. "That looks just like the beetle in the suitcase."

"I think it IS our beetle!" Chase exclaims.

"But ours doesn't have those tiny pictures painted on the bottom," Ava says, pointing.

"We don't know that," Chase says.

"Only one way to find out," Ava says. As soon as she opens the lid, they have their answer!

The beetle has popped out of its slot and is lying upside down. Tiny symbols painted in gold run along the bottom.

"These pictures are an ancient Egyptian language called hieroglyphics," Chase explains. "I bet I can figure out what the pictures on our beetle mean!" He quickly flips to the back of his book. His eyes dart back and forth between the beetle and a chart.

"Well? What do the pictures say?" Ava asks.

Then he looks up, eyes round. "They say: **Tut-ankh-amun, ruler of upper Annu**! Tutankhamun is King Tut's full name! This beetle must belong to King Tut!"

Chase has been fascinated with the young king ever since visiting the Egyptian wing at the museum. "King Tut might have touched this!" he says, grabbing the beetle.

"Ahhh!" Ava yelps, throwing both arms around her brother's leg.

Chase looks at her in surprise. Then, with a sinking feeling, he realizes what he has done.

AGAIN.

Deserts Are HOT

When the spinning stops, Chase and Ava are sprawled on the sand.

"I can't believe I picked up the beetle!" Chase groans. "All our supplies are still at home!" He shoves the history book into his back pocket, then pushes the beetle into Ava's hand. "I don't trust myself with it."

She slides the beetle into a pocket in her tutu.

"Why are you so hard on yourself?" Ava asks. "I make mistakes all the time."

"Well, I don't," Chase replies.

She grins. "Trust me, big brother. It gets easier."

"Great," he mutters. But he does feel a little better.

"Besides, we are still more prepared than before," she points out. "We have both our canteens, your book, and the beetle. There's no sandstorm and I don't see any deadly scorpions. So things aren't *all* bad."

"I guess you're right," Chase says. "We're in ancient Egypt, after all. And we could meet King Tut!"

They look in the distance and can see some pyramids, with tents set up among them. "That must be some kind of ancient marketplace," Chase says. "Like our flea market."

"Let's check it out!" Ava says.

The hot sun beats down as they trudge through the heavy sand.

They've just gulped from their canteens when Ava shouts, "Something is coming toward us!"

Chase squints into the sun and darts in front of his sister. A giant creature with brown fur, four long legs, and two humps stops in front of them.

It's a camel! Chase doesn't relax yet. Who knows if camels are friendly?

This one must be used to people because it kneels down like it wants them to get on its back! A leather saddle has been set up between the two humps.

Ava claps. "I've always wanted to ride a camel!" She climbs up and grabs the reins.

Chase is NOT getting up there. That animal looks very wobbly!

Ava leans back in the saddle. "Come on. It's a lot faster than walking."

"Nope," Chase replies.

"What if King Tut is at that marketplace right now?" she says. "I bet once we return his beetle, you two will become best friends!"

Chase scrambles up onto the camel. What's a little wobbliness when he's about to become best friends with KING TUT?!

Over the Hump

Chase gets more and more excited as he and Ava near the first pyramid. They hear voices and tools clanging, but don't see any workers yet.

The camel stops and kneels down. They slide off onto the sand. Ava pats it on the nose. "Thank you, camel friend."

"Let's go check out the marketplace!" Chase says.

"A yummy ancient Egyptian snack would be nice!" Ava adds.

But when they reach the other side of the pyramid, there are no booths offering old books or colorful woven baskets. Instead, they find wooden crates marked FRAGILE, shovels, axes, men pushing wheelbarrows, and at least ten giant pits in the ground.

Each pit has two or three workers chipping away at stones or brushing off dried sand.

There is a tent beside each pit, which must be where the workers sleep. Chase can see foldable beds inside with a wooden trunk at the foot of each.

FRAGILE

A table covered in papers, maps, and half-empty coffee cups sits a few feet away from Chase and Ava.

"I don't understand. Ancient Egypt was, like, three thousand years ago," Ava says. "But they didn't have all this stuff way back then. . . ."

Chase reaches for a newspaper on the table and sees today's date: November 4, 1922. "We're not in ancient Egypt after all! We never were."

"Well," Ava says, "at least we're not wearing sheets as robes then, right?"

"I guess," Chase mutters. So much for being best friends with King Tut!

Two men carrying tools and clipboards step out of a nearby tent. Chase and Ava duck down behind the table.

"We've looked everywhere for King Tut's tomb, but we haven't found anything," one man grumbles. "Carter is going to call off the search soon."

The name *Carter* sounds familiar. . . .

Once the men pass, Chase pulls out his history book.

"Here it is. November fourth, 1922! Today is the day that British archaeologist Howard *Carter* discovers King Tut's tomb!" Chase says. "Archaeologists dig for ancient buried treasures! We must be in the Valley of the Kings! Lots of ancient Egyptian rulers are buried here — in underground rooms called tombs. The pyramids were built on top of them. The only tomb still full of treasures was King Tut's! We're in the middle of the most famous archaeological dig in history!"

chapter 8

Tents for Tut

Ava pulls Chase into the nearest tent. "It's cool we might get to see King Tut's tomb being discovered," she says, "but I thought we had to give the king the beetle. What do we do with it now?"

Chase flips to the page in his book that showed the jeweled beetle. "It says here that a water boy spotted the beetle in a pile of rubble and told Howard Carter about it. That's how Carter found stairs leading to King Tut's tomb," he explains. "Our beetle belongs in that pile of rubble. We need to make sure someone finds it there today — or King Tut's tomb will never be discovered!"

"Let's get going then! We need to find that rubble pile!" Ava says, darting out of the tent.

Chase pulls her back in. "Wait! We need to look like we belong here."

"Right," Ava says, frowning down at her tutu.

"How about this?" Chase points to a big canvas bag marked LAUNDRY.

Ava picks up a crumpled sock and wrinkles her nose. "Yuck."

All the clothes they pull out are covered in a layer of dirt. But once Ava rolls up the pant legs and shirtsleeves, the clothes fit well enough. Ava hides her tutu in the laundry bag. She grabs a brown wide-brimmed hat and throws a matching one to Chase. It's large enough to hide his dino hat.

"Now we look like real archaeologists," Ava declares. "We're ready to dig up ancient treasures!"

"If only we knew where to go," Chase says.

Ava turns Chase around. A map is taped to the side of the tent behind him. "I am pretty sure *this* map is not upside down," she says.

"That'll work!" Chase says with a grin. The map shows detailed drawings of the entire dig site. All the pits and pyramids are neatly labeled.

They quickly find a large pile of rubble near a tomb marked RAMSES VI.

"There it is!" Ava cries.

Unwelcome Guest

"Let's go put this beetle where it belongs!" Chase says with a rush of excitement.

Ava grabs a shovel and hands him a clipboard. "Here. These will help us blend in."

Chase waves the clipboard in the air. "Why do I get a lame clipboard and you get a cool shovel?"

"Do you want to switch?" Ava asks.

"Nah," he says with a grin. "The shovel looks heavy."

Ava rolls her eyes. She grabs a handful of mushy grapes before following him out.

Exciting things are happening in every direction! Archaeologists hunch over open pits. Some chisel stone. Some use brushes to gently wipe sand off newly discovered objects. Statues and painted urns and pottery are lined up in neat rows, waiting to be cleaned off.

"Think about it," Chase says as they hurry toward the tomb of Ramses VI. "All this stuff had been buried for thousands of years. Imagine what's hiding underneath our feet!"

Ava stops walking and points to a wooden sign: TOMB OF RAMSES VI.

"King Tut himself might be under our feet!" she says. "This is the place!"

"And that must be the rubble pile we're looking for," Chase says, pointing at a pile of rocks, dirt, wooden boards, and broken tools near the tomb's entrance. "Let's go put the beetle where it belongs."

Ava goes pale. "Uh-oh," she says, feeling her pants pockets. "I left the beetle in my tutu!" She turns to run back to the tent to get it.

"Wait!" Chase says, grabbing hold of her arm. "Look."

A tall man is leaning against the side of the pyramid near where Ramses's tomb is located. At first, he looks like any other archaeologist taking a break from digging. He has a hat over his face, like he is sleeping standing up. But something about him looks familiar. . . .

They have seen this man before, and it wasn't in Egypt.

Randall!

Randall Returns!

chapter 10

"Randall should still be locked up in King Arthur's dungeon! How did he get out?" Ava demands.

Chase wipes his sweaty brow. The air feels even hotter now. "Randall must have had his remote with him. That's the only way he could have escaped. And then he tracked us here somehow."

Ava kicks the sand. "He'll see us if we try to drop the beetle now. And what if he tries to take it from us?"

"We can't let that happen," Chase says.

A pair of workmen digging nearby begin arguing over a broken bowl.

"That was priceless!" one man shouts. "You stepped on it!"

"I'm sorry!" the other replies. "I didn't see it!"

Randall rubs his eyes. He looks over at the arguing men — and spots Chase and Ava!

He springs toward them.

Chase and
Ava only have time
to duck around the side
of the pyramid before he
catches up to them. They're
trapped!

"Give me the beetle," Randall demands,
holding out his palm. "NOW."

Ava throws down her shovel and lifts her
chin. "We don't have it," she replies.

"You couldn't have gotten here without
it," he growls.

"Maybe we got here the same way you did," Chase says, hoping to trick Randall into giving away his secrets.

"Impossible," Randall snaps. "I'm not a Time Jumper!"

"What *is* a Time Jumper?" Ava asks.

"You two don't understand anything," Randall hisses.

"We understand some things!" Chase shouts. "We know you are trying to mess up history!"

"Enough!" Randall roars. "Just give me the beetle!" He lunges for them but trips over Ava's shovel and gets a face full of sand!

He tries to get up, but Chase lobs his clipboard at him.

"Oomph!" Randall slides right back down onto the sand. "I'll be guarding that pile all day! You'll never be able to drop off the beetle!"

"Don't worry," Chase tells Ava as they run away. "We'll figure something out."

When they reach the tent, the place feels emptier.

Ava whirls around. "Where's the laundry bag?"

Chase's heart skips a beat. "It was right here!"

The laundry bag *and* the beetle are GONE!

Underground Hideout

There aren't many places for a laundry bag to hide. Still, Chase and Ava search every inch of the tent.

"Maybe someone collected it to do the wash?" Chase suggests.

They rush out of the tent and bump right into a workman pulling a wooden cart.

"Oh, sorry," Ava says, stepping out of the way.

Then Chase gasps. Five bags of laundry are piled in the cart! "Wait!" he calls out to the workman. "We need to get something from our bag."

The man shrugs. "Hurry up."

Chase and Ava tear through all five bags. Luckily, a tie-dyed tutu is easy to spot!

Ava grabs the beetle out of the pocket, then shoves the tutu back into the bag.

She chuckles as the workman rolls his cart away. "Someone will get a fun surprise when their laundry comes back."

"Come on," Chase says. "I know a place we can go to keep an eye on Randall. Maybe he'll fall asleep again and we can sneak back to the rubble pile."

He leads Ava to the pyramid across from Ramses VI's tomb. It has two entrances — one looks right out at Randall!

Ava's eyes light up. "We're going to hide inside a pyramid?"

Chase nods. "I warn you though, we might stumble across a dead mummy or two!"

She grins. "I'll race you!"

They tumble over each other in their rush to enter the pyramid first. They both shiver when they get inside. The air must be thirty degrees cooler!

Every wall is painted with hieroglyphics and drawings of people and animals and boats and birds. No dead mummies though, which Chase at least is happy about.

Ava points up to the high ceiling, which is also full of artwork. She pulls out her camera and snaps a picture. "Wow."

"Double wow," Chase replies.

They wander around until they've seen everything in the huge room.

Chase peers out the back doorway. "Randall's still there," he says. "He really is guarding that rubble pile."

Ava groans. "Doesn't this guy ever need to go to the bathroom?"

"The sun is starting to go down," Chase says. "Remember: The history book said this beetle has to be discovered *today*. We have to go right now, before it's too late."

"Time Jumpers on the move!" Ava shouts and darts outside.

X Marks the Spot

"Wait!" Chase says, pulling Ava back into the doorway of the pyramid. "Look! Randall's not alone anymore!"

A very tall archaeologist is shouting at Randall. "You're not being paid to stand around! We need help over in Pit Number Four. Now!"

Randall tries to argue, but eventually follows the man away.

"This is our chance!" Chase whispers. Ava nods and they dash over to the rubble pile as soon as the coast is clear.

"*You* should put the beetle in the pile," Ava says, pushing it into Chase's hands.

"We should do it together," he says. "That is what worked with King Arthur's sword."

Ava nods.

They each hold on to an end of the beetle and set it down in the center of the pile.

Chase waits for that feeling of time slowing that he'd felt last time, but it doesn't come. No colorful glow surrounds the beetle like it did with the sword either.

"It's not working! What did we do wrong?" Ava asks.

Chase frowns. "Leaving it here must not be good enough. My book said a local water boy was the first person to spot the beetle. Maybe our job isn't done until *he* sees it. But how do we find a water boy?"

Ava points to a group of boys carrying buckets of water toward one of the pits.

"Okay, that was easier than I thought it would be," Chase says. "But we can't just walk up and ask, 'Hey, who wants to see a cool beetle made of stone?' I mean, no one actually *likes* beetles."

"*I* like them!" Ava protests. "And the ancient Egyptians sure did. They painted beetles all over the inside of that pyramid we just hid in. Come on. I'll do the talking."

Ava walks over and taps the last boy in line. "Do any of you like beetles?"

Water sloshes from the boy's bucket as he points at a smaller boy up ahead. A large beetle is sitting on the boy's shoulder! And he's smiling down at it!

Ava nudges Chase and whispers, "I think that's our water boy!"

Skreeee!! A shrill whistle slices through the air. The sound makes Chase and Ava jump, and the small beetle flies off the boy's shoulder.

The archaeologists lay down their shovels and brushes. One of them throws his hat on the ground with a grunt. Chase recognizes him from the photograph in his book: Howard Carter!

"What's going on?" Chase asks the water boy.

"The whistle means the search for King Tut's tomb has ended," the boy says sadly. "I had hoped we would find it."

"Come on! The day isn't over!" Ava says, tugging the boy toward the pile of rubble. "Don't give up yet."

Chase follows, keeping an eye out for Randall. He's bound to show up any second now that the work is over.

"I'm Ava," she tells the boy as they run. "And this is my brother, Chase."

"I am called Amon," the boy replies.

"I think you'll like this, Amon," Ava says when they reach the pile. She points at their beetle, which still rests on top of the pile.

Amon quickly reaches for it. "A jeweled scarab beetle! I have never seen one so beautiful! This is priceless!"

Amon turns and shouts, "Mr. Carter! Mr. Carter! Come see what I found!"

Mr. Carter comes running over, but from out of nowhere, Randall shows up and darts in front of him!

"That beetle belongs to ME!" Randall shouts, reaching out to grab it from Amon.

Amon closes his hand over it just in time. Then in one swift move, he darts between Randall's legs and thrusts the beetle at Mr. Carter!

"What is all this fuss about?" Mr. Carter says, holding the beetle up to inspect it. He makes a choking sound when he reads the hieroglyphics on the bottom. His whole face lights up!

At that instant, a green glow surrounds the beetle and Mr. Carter. A delicious tingle runs down Chase's back, and just for one second, things around them move in slow motion before snapping back. He and Ava grin at each other. They did it!

Randall is so angry that his face has turned purple!

Mr. Carter bends down to Amon. "You found this here? In this exact spot?" he asks.

Amon nods.

Mr. Carter holds the beetle high over his head. "We've finally found the sign we've been searching for!" he shouts. "This beetle has writing on it that tells us it belonged to King Tut! We must dig here right away!"

Ava snaps a picture of the joyful archaeologist. Workers come running from all directions, cheering and whooping.

Chase pulls Ava away from the crowd. "We'd better get back home. Randall looks ready to explode."

"Is the remote buzzing?" Ava asks.

"How should I know?" Chase says. "Didn't you grab it before we left my bedroom?"

She shakes her head. "I barely had time to grab *you*!"

They stare at each other as the truth sinks in.

They'd left the remote at home!

Trapped in Time!

Chase and Ava dash back into the pyramid they'd hidden in earlier.

Her voice shaking, Ava asks, "Are we stuck here forever? The magic remote is what brought us back from King Arthur's castle! How will we get home without it? I'd miss Mom and Dad and my friends and school and my bike! And cheese doodles haven't even been invented yet!"

Leave it to Ava to think about snack foods at this moment. As much as Chase loves history, he doesn't want to live a hundred years in the past either. Maybe if they were back in prehistoric times with dinosaurs that would be a different story.

Randall storms right past the doorway of the pyramid without spotting them. He pulls something out of his pocket. It's his remote! And the red button is flashing!

Chase pulls on Ava's sleeve. "Come on! This is our chance to get back home!"

They race after Randall, catching up right as he is about to press the button.

"Wait!" Ava shouts at him.

Randall drops the remote in surprise, then swiftly scoops it back out of the sand before Chase or Ava can reach it. "Have you two finally come to your senses and decided to give me the suitcase?"

"We don't have it with us," Chase says.

Randall looks at Chase's empty hands and then at Ava's. A smile creeps across his face. "It looks like that's not the only thing you don't have with you. No one can travel through time without a remote — not even Time Jumpers. I guess it's my turn to leave *you* back in time!"

"You wouldn't!" Ava shouts.

He presses the button.

The Egyptian Wing

Chase and Ava both fling themselves at Randall's legs. They catch the bottom of his pants just as the sand beneath them falls away. Chase is afraid Randall is going to try to kick them off as they swirl around, but he doesn't seem to know they'd latched on!

■ 79 ■

Seconds later, they find themselves on a hard, shiny floor surrounded by statues and display cases covered in glass. They are definitely *not* back at home!

Chase and Ava immediately let go of Randall's pants and scramble to hide behind the nearest statue. They hold their breath as Randall lurches to his feet. He gives a quick glance around him, then stops in front of one of the glass display cases. He scowls at something before hurrying across the large room. They quickly lose sight of him.

OSIRIS

Chase breathes a sigh of relief. They're safe! But where are they?

Chase looks up at the ancient Egyptian statue they are crouching behind.

Ava frowns. "Are we still in Egypt?" she asks.

"I'm not sure," Chase says. "I think I've been here before. . . ."

A family walks by in modern clothes and it hits him. "We're in the Egyptian wing of the Natural History Museum!" Chase says. "We're back in our own town — and in our time!"

Ava whirls around. "Look, Chase!" She points at black-and-white photographs that show the discovery of King Tut's tomb. "There's Amon — and Mr. Carter. And those are the backs of our heads!"

Chase leans in closer. "We're actually a part of history!"

"And so is our beetle!" Ava says, her face pressed up against the glass of a nearby display case.

Sure enough, the green-jeweled beetle is on display.

A priceless jeweled scarab beetle found at the entrance to King Tut's tomb

"Why do you think we landed in the museum?" Chase asks.

"Randall must have been visiting when he time traveled," Ava says. "That's why his remote brought him back here."

"I don't think he was *visiting*," Chase says, pointing at a door across the room marked EMPLOYEE EXIT. Randall is holding a card up to a sensor next to the door. A light on the sensor turns from red to green. He pushes on the door handle and slips out the door.

Chase and Ava stare after him. Randall — the man who is trying to mess up history — WORKS AT THE HISTORY MUSEUM??

The Long Road Home

chapter 16

Chase and Ava walk down the museum's big front steps.

"I don't get it," Chase says as they make their way to the sidewalk. "The whole point of a museum is to save history and to teach people about it. Not to ruin it! I can't believe Randall *works* here!"

"I'm too tired and thirsty to think about that now," Ava says.

But Chase can't stop thinking about Randall. He keeps talking. "And Randall was wrong about one thing at least. We *are* able to time travel without the remote — well, sort of. When my hand first grazed the beetle."

"You're right," she says. "But I'm too tired to think about that either."

Chase tries to ignore the looks they're getting from people on the street. It's hard to blend in when you're dressed like 1920s archaeologists and covered in a layer of sand and dirt!

Sand falls off them with each tired step.

Mom spots them as they walk up their driveway. "I thought you two were upstairs. Whose clothes are those? And why are you so dirty?"

"Um," Chase says. Ava stays silent.

"They're playing nicely together," Dad says, coming out of the garage with a half-finished sculpture under his arm. "That's good enough for me."

Chase and Ava smile as Mom squints at them. "Fine. But go get cleaned up before lunch."

They dash into the house before she can change her mind.

"I can't believe it's not even lunchtime yet!" Ava says as they climb the stairs.

"I know," Chase says. "Time travel is so weird."

The backpack with their supplies is still on the bed. Chase digs in it and pulls out two granola bars. They're too hungry to wait for lunch to eat.

"Good thing Mom and Dad didn't come in here while we were gone," Ava says, chomping on hers. "We left the suitcase wide open." She swings the lid closed and slides the suitcase under the bed.

"I was thinking," Chase says, "if Madeline's uncle worked at the museum before he disappeared, and if Randall works there now . . . maybe her uncle and Randall know each other. We should ask Madeline."

Ava shakes her head. "Madeline didn't seem to want to talk about Randall. Remember?"

"Good point," Chase says. "Then let's ask Mom and Dad to take us back to the museum tomorrow. We can ask around."

"I think we might be busy tomorrow," Ava says.

"Really?" Chase asks. "Why?"

She points below them. "Don't you hear it?"

"Oh nooo . . ." he says. They peek under the bed. Sure enough . . .

Rattle rattle. Rattle rattle.

WENDY MASS

has written several award-winning series for young readers including the **Willow Falls** series, *Twice Upon a Time*, *Space Taxi*, and *The Candymakers*. She recently learned that you can travel back in time every night just by looking up at the sky! The light from stars takes so long to reach us that any star you see is in the past. How cool is that? Wendy and her family live in a rural part of New Jersey. They have two cats and a dog, all of whom she calls her son's name by mistake.

ORIOL VIDAL

is an illustrator and storyboard artist who lives in Barcelona, Spain, with his wife, daughter, and a cat named Lana. He always wanted to be a "painter" when he grew up. Finally, his hobby became his job! Time Jumpers is the first early chapter book series he has illustrated. When Oriol is not drawing, he likes to travel with his family all over the world. And in his dreams, he time travels to the past . . . just like the Time Jumpers!

Time Jumpers

Questions and Activities

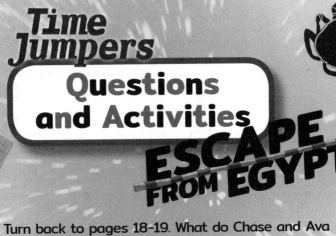

ESCAPE FROM EGYPT

1 Turn back to pages 18-19. What do Chase and Ava learn about Madeline's uncle?

2 What will happen if the Time Jumpers do not return the scarab beetle in time? Turn back to page 42.

3 Chase and Ava leave an important time-travel object at home. What is it and why do they need it?

4 Turn back to pages 44-45. This map uses a counting system called **Roman numerals**. Using the Internet, look up how to write numbers 1 through 10 in Roman numerals. Chase and Ava are looking for the tomb of Ramses VI. What number is VI?

5 Chase and Ava disguise themselves as **archaeologists**. Look up what archaeologists are and what they do. If you were an archaeologist, what would you want to discover?